F

Golden Corn

Story Keeper Series
Book 6

Dave and Pat Sargent (*left*) are longtime residents of Prairie Grove, Arkansas. Dave, a fourth-generation dairy farmer, began writing in early December 1990. Pat, a former teacher, began writing in the fourth grade. They enjoy the outdoors and have a real love for animals.

Sue Rogers (*right*) returned to her beloved Mississippi after retirement. She shared books with children for more than thirty years. These stories fulfill a dream of writing books—to continue the sharing

Fields of Golden Corn

Story Keeper Series
Book 6

By Dave and Pat Sargent
and Sue Rogers

Beyond "The End"
By Sue Rogers

Illustrated by Jane Lenoir

Ozark Publishing, Inc.
P.O. Box 228
Prairie Grove, AR 72753

Cataloging-in-Publication Data

Sargent, Dave,1941–
    Fields of golden corn / by Dave and
Pat Sargent and Sue Rogers ; illustrated by
Jane Lenoir. —Prairie Grove, AR : Ozark
Publishing, c2004.
        p. cm. (Story keeper series ; 6)

        "Be energetic"—Cover.
    SUMMARY: The person who first
causes a Navajo child to laugh out loud will
play an important role in his life. How will
Grandfather influence Bidziil?
        ISBN 1-56763-913-5 (hc)
                1-56763-914-3 (pbk)

        1. Indians of North America—Juvenile
fiction. 2. Navajo Indians—Juvenile fiction.
[1. Native Americans—United States—Fiction.
2. Navajo Indians—Fiction] 1. Sargent,
Pat, 1936– II. Rogers, Sue, 1933– III. Lenoir,
Jane, 1950– ill. IV. Title. V. Series

    PZ7.S243Fi 2004
    [Fic]—dc21   2003091115

Copyright © 2004 by Dave and Pat Sargent
and Sue Rogers
All rights reserved
Printed in the United States of America

Inspired by
the four majestic mountains
that enclose the Navajo land.

Dedicated to
Leonard,
a wonderful husband,
proud father, and loving PawPaw.

Foreword
Bidziil learned to live in harmony and beauty. He learned the ways of his people through stories and string games told by his grandfather. He learned to cherish and respect the Navajo's land. He explored the steep sandstone-capped mesas and buttes and the broad sandy valleys. He learned ways of fringe-toed lizards and shovel-nosed snakes. He also learned a lesson about snow storms!

Contents

If you would like to have the authors of the Story Keeper Series visit your school free of charge, just call us at 1-800-321-5671 or 1-800-960-3876.

One

My Smallest Son

The day I was born, my mother put her cheek close to mine. In a firm yet gentle voice, she spoke these words to me, "Become a leader, my smallest son, strong and stern like the invincible mountain."

My cradleboard was made of cottonwood. It was laced together with thin strips of leather. The flat boards helped make my back strong and straight. The cradleboard was blessed with corn pollen, prayers, songs, and good thoughts.

My mother grew golden corn. She knew that her corn needed four things—sunlight, water, air, and soil. She also knew that her young son needed four values—values of life, of work, of social and human relations, and of respect and reverence. My mother took care of her corn. She took care of her son.

Laughter filled our hogan. My mother often sang a song,

"All is beautiful before me,
All is beautiful behind me,
All is beautiful above me,
All is beautiful around me."

Each song or chant was a prayer to the Holy People. The word *hozho* at the end was a reminder to live in harmony and beauty. My mother made our hogan a beautiful happy place.

One night my shicheii (my grandfather) was playing with me.

He was chanting a little verse and wiggling one toe at a time. It tickled. I laughed out loud!

My family began gathering around. The first time a Navajo child laughs out loud is a time for honor and celebration. We had a laughing party. Everyone sat around me. They ate sweet corn cake and played with me.

"You were the first to make Bidziil laugh, my husband," said my shimasani (my grandmother). "You will play an important role in his life."

"I will teach shi'tsoi (my grandson) many things," said Grandfather.

My family lived in a hogan made of cedar logs, covered with mud, sod, and bark. It was round and cone shaped. The ceiling inside was domed with peeled logs, and had a smoke hole at the top.

"My smallest son, look up into the tall cribbed ceiling and know that Father Sky is covering you and is protecting you," crooned my mother. "Soon your little bare feet will feel Mother Earth supporting you and nourishing you on our earthen floor."

The door of our hogan faced

east to meet the rising sun. The hogan and the family greeted Father Sun the first thing in the morning.

"Good morning, Father Sun," we said.

We also made offerings of corn pollen to each dawn. We prayed to the spirits of the sacred mountains. A fire stick beside the door protected us from evil spirits and wicked men.

We lived in a female hogan. The fire was warm and inviting. It warmed the family and cooked our food. It was a healthy safe place for my family. I learned early that the hogan was a blend of the harmony of my people and our spiritual universe.

There were smaller hogans in our village, male hogans. Their doors looked like tunnels.

Many of the ceremonies took place in the male hogan. This is where enemies were met, and where healing rituals took place. Unlike the friendly fire in family hogans, this ceremonial fire was very dangerous.

Two

More Than Entertainment

My mother told me stories to teach me patience and how to be a good person. The stories my grandmother told me were about animals. Coyote tried to outsmart others in order to get what he wanted. His plans usually backfired.

But my grandfather, who was an elder, taught me through stories how my people, the *Dine* (Navajo), came to be. His stories taught me how to live. He told me how to have a good life. He told me how I must learn to balance my needs, my people's needs, nature, and the spirits.

My favorite stories were about Spider Man and Spider Woman. Spider Man taught the Navajos how to make a loom from sunshine, rain, and lightning.

I never tired of hearing how Spider Woman taught the women to weave.

I would sit for hours and watch Grandmother in front of a large wooden loom. She would pass a wooden stick in and out between strands of thread.

"Grandmother, why do you leave a hole in the middle of each blanket?" I asked.

"Oh, my child," Grandmother would say, "I must leave a hole. If I do not, my weaving thoughts will be trapped in the threads. It will bring bad luck. It will drive me mad! Now, run along and learn how to make an arrow. We may need a nice fat rabbit for a stew."

"Have you heard the story of how Spider Woman helped a Navajo boy escape from his enemy?" asked Grandfather.

"No, Grandfather," I answered.

"When he came to the tall sides of Spider Rock, there was no place left to run. Spider Woman let down a web. The boy quickly climbed up the web and lost his enemy. He was fed eagle eggs and drank the night's dew on top of the rock! That is how he survived."

It was no trouble for my grandfather to get me to behave. He only
had to remind me that Spider Woman
would let down her web, carry me up
to her home, and devour me!

Many of Grandfather's stories were told with the help of a string.

Spider Woman taught the Dine string games. These string figures were not just games for us to play. They taught us to help keep our thinking in order. We kept our lives in order with the stories. Winter was a time of year when spiders were not present. So people could play string games in the winter. We never played our string games in front of the summer and spring Holy Beings. That time is when the string was untied, washed, and then given back to the Holy People.

"Never play string games in the summer, Bidziil," my grandfather said. "It will cause bad weather and bad luck. Besides, Spider Woman will tie your eyes shut!"

18

Three

No Backyard Fences

"Come on, Bidziil," called my cousin one cold day. "Let's get our friends and do some roaming!"

My cousin, Nastas, and I had seen eight winters. We had seen many miles of broad sandy valleys and steep sandstone-capped mesas and buttes in our vast backyard. We climbed mountains and crossed deep canyons. We chased fringe-toed lizards across sand dunes and watched shovel-nosed snakes burrow through the sand. We swam and fished in rivers and lakes. We roamed around under the burning sun and in driving rain. Neither great winds nor snow made a fence for us!

Our mothers' fields of corn were the closest thing to a fence. We were welcome in the fields, but not to play.

Two friends joined us. The cold winds of Nil chiihtsoh were blowing strong today, so I added one of Grandmother's blankets across my shoulder. This was the time when Spider Woman was asleep, so I put my string in a pouch and a handful of roasted corn. Nastas was always hungry, so I added another handful of corn. We were off.

There was a big mule deer that made his home on one of the red, flat-topped mesas across the canyon. He had large antlers. He liked to eat acorns from the oak trees there. When winter snows began to fall, he found a trail into the juniper forest below. We decided to see if he was still up there eating acorns. The snows would begin soon.

The snows began sooner than we thought. We had climbed to the top of the mesa and walked to the far end where the sides were steep and perpendicular. There was no sign of the deer.

Snow began to fall—the first snow. What fun!

Our fun soon ended. The wind whipped snow across our hands and faces. It felt like tiny knives. We could hardly see one another.

There we were on top of a mesa with three steep sides. There was only one way down, and in this snowstorm, we couldn't see which way that was! What were we going to do? We were afraid.

Suddenly, Grandfather's voice began singing in my mind. It was calm and strong.

"Always remember, my grandson, the Earth is your mother. She will give you knowledge," the warm memory said. "Ask the yei-bi-chei (the grandfather spirits) to watch over you."

"Come quick," I called to my friends. "We will sit together under this tree until the storm passes. Make a square, facing one another."

Struggling with the strong wind, we spread Grandmother's blanket

over our heads. Then we sat on the
blanket corners, huddled together.

The blanket's dome made it feel almost like we were in our hogan. It gave a feeling of balance. We could open our eyes and look at each other. Nastas helped more when he looked at us and said his familiar words, "I'm hungry!"

"Here is some corn. There will be enough for each of us to have a few kernels," I said, digging in my pouch. "We will stay here tonight. This storm should be over by dawn. We can see our way home. I brought my string. Would you like to hear some stories it tells?" Grandfather's voice guided me through the stories as I used my loop of string. We were cold, but we felt safe.

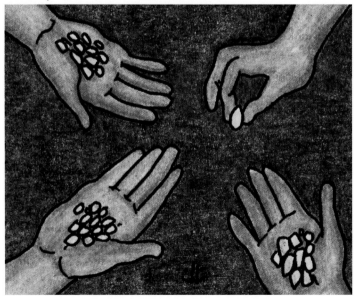

The others went to sleep. I munched on my corn.

Memories of my mother storing the alastsli (seed) for another year's planting floated by. I could clearly see her preparing a fertile ground, and hear her voice asking the spirits to bless her work.

After her prayer, I could see her take four kernels of corn and plant one each at the north, at the south, at the east, and at the west sides of the first hill. Then clouds darkened the sky, thunder rolled, and lightning flashed. The rain poured down. This was the male rain. The female rain was gentle. The sun and rain made fields of golden corn—to nourish my mother's family and pollen for use in ceremonies and prayer offerings.

I was tasting my mother's kneel-down bread and blue corn mush as I slowly drifted off to sleep.

The very next thing I heard was, "I'm hungry!" Nastas was awake. Now we were all awake. The snow was heavy on our backs. The winds were quiet! We stood and shook great piles of snow from the blanket.

It was a sunny day. We found our way home.

Songs, thanksgiving prayers, corn pollen, and plenty of warm hugs greeted me. Thick corn soup with kneel-down bread filled my stomach. I told my mother how memories of her fields of golden corn had warmed me through the cold night.

"Grandfather, I want to be an elder just like you. I have learned how important the stories are to our people. I want to lead the children, to teach them our ways through stories. Thank you for inspiring me. Will you teach me more?" I asked.

"Yes, my grandson," said Grandfather proudly. "And I may tickle your toes again!"

Four

Navajo Facts

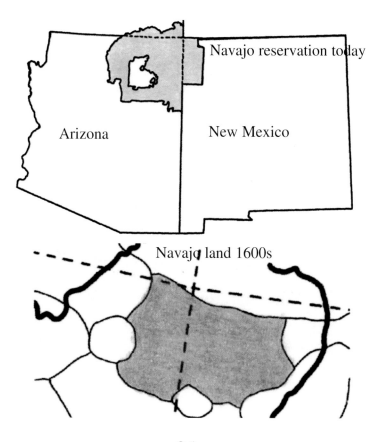

Navajo reservation today

Arizona

New Mexico

Navajo land 1600s

Navajo weaving

Churro sheep are very rare. They have four horns and
some babies are born with spots. The sheep can be
many colors. The spots usually fade to a solid color.
Churro sheep came from the Spanish. The sheep have
fine wool with very little oil which makes it good for
extremely fine weavings. The breed almost died out in
the early 1800s when the United States cavalry round-
ed up all the Navajos, burned their orchards and fields,
killed their sheep, and marched them 300 miles to east-
ern New Mexico. There the Navajos were held captive
at Fort Apache for several years. They were allowed
to go back to their territory when no gold was found.

Chief's Blanket

Navajo weaving

32

Sites on Navajo reservation

Monument Valley

Window Rock

Spider Rock

Massacre Cave

Spider Rock,
aerial view

Navajo craft

Kokopeli silver buckle

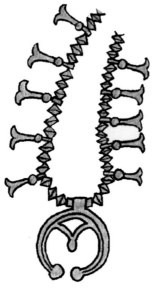

Squash blossom necklace

Pendant

Spider-Woman basket

Ring

34

Navajo craft

Basket

Pottery

Rattle

Knife and scabbard

Navajo pictographs from Arizona and New Mexico

Anasazi-style deer

Sun God

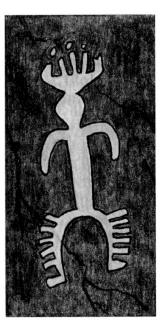

Crane with frog

Spirit figure

Beyond "The End"

● Bidziil's mother wanted him to be strong and stern like the **invincible** mountain. This is a mighty BIG word. When I looked it up, I found it is a very powerful word also that means "incapable of being conquered, defeated, or subdued."

Bidziil's mother wanted him to grow up to be a strong and powerful man, didn't she? Look up the definitions of these words if you do not know what they mean.

Write a paragraph about someone you think is **invincible**. Describe this person.

37

CURRICULUM CONNECTIONS

● On the Navajo Reservation today, there are many weavers. Some of them are men. They are most famous for weaving rugs now. Read about the Navajo weavers. Look at their designs.

Bidziil's grandmother made her yarn and dyed it herself. If you boil onion skins in a little water, you will get a reddish brown. Boil some marigolds for a yellow. What color would you get from beets? Experiment with other materials. Ask an adult to boil the materials you gather. Dye some white cotton strips in the colored water—or, hey, you can tie dye a cool t-shirt!

● To which cultural group do the Navajo people belong?

- They have the largest reservation in the United States. Where is it? What are the names of the four mountains that mark its boundaries?
- Wherever corn is grown, children make cornhusk dolls. You can make one for yourself. Instructions are at website <www. teachersfirst.com/summer/cornhusk.htm>.
- The number four was important to the Navajo. How many things can you think of that comes in sets of four: the directions north, south, east, west; the four seasons; or the four sacred stones?

THE ARTS

● Navajo sandpaintings originated with the Holy People. They were, and still are, mainly ceremonial. Read about how the medicine men used sandpaintings for healing.

Today many artists create sand-painting pictures and textiles to sell. Sandpainting is not forbidden as long as Holy People are not pictured.

Create a sandpainting of your own. There is a pattern with good instruc-tions at website <www.maingfriends. com/sandart_native_american.htm>.

GATHERING INFORMATION

● We call corn—*corn*. However, the Germanic form is *korn*, and the Latin form is *grain*. Most of the Native American tribes use the term *maize*—or was that just in movies, books, or plays?

Do they actually use *maize*, or do they say *corn*? It is time for some research! See what kind of information you can gather! By the way, the Aztec called it *centli* and to the Maya it was *cor*.

THE BEST I CAN BE

● Bidziil's mother took care that her son developed the four values: the value of life, the value of work, the value of social and human relations, and the value of respect and reverence.

What do the "values of life" mean to you; the "values of work"; the "values of social and human relations"; and the "values of respect and reverence"?